W9-ACU-668

Ada Lace

and the
Impossible Mission

ALSO BY EMILY CALANDRELLI

Ada Lace, on the Case
Ada Lace Sees Red
Ada Lace, Take Me to Your Leader

Ada Lace

and the Impossible Mission

· AN ADA LACE ADVENTURE ·

EMILY CALANDRELLI

with TAMSON WESTON

ILLUSTRATED BY RENÉE KURILLA

Simon & Schuster Books for Young Readers

New York London Toronto Sydney New Delhi

*For the kids who let their curiosity get the best
of them—it will create the best in you*
—E. C.

For Keith Zoo, my partner in crime
—R. K.

SIMON & SCHUSTER BOOKS FOR YOUNG READERS
An imprint of Simon & Schuster Children's Publishing Division
1230 Avenue of the Americas, New York, New York 10020
This book is a work of fiction. Any references to historical events,
real people, or real places are used fictitiously. Other names, characters, places,
and events are products of the author's imagination, and any resemblance to actual
events or places or persons, living or dead, is entirely coincidental.
Text copyright © 2018 by Emily Calandrelli
Jacket and interior illustrations copyright © 2018 by Renée Kurilla
All rights reserved, including the right of reproduction in whole or in part in any form.
SIMON & SCHUSTER BOOKS FOR YOUNG READERS
is a trademark of Simon & Schuster, Inc.
For information about special discounts for bulk purchases, please contact Simon &
Schuster Special Sales at 1-866-506-1949 or business@simonandschuster.com.
The Simon & Schuster Speakers Bureau can bring authors to your live event. For more
information or to book an event, contact the Simon & Schuster Speakers Bureau
at 1-866-248-3049 or visit our website at www.simonspeakers.com.
Also available in a Simon & Schuster Books for Young Readers paperback edition
Book design by Laurent Linn
The text for this book was set in Minister Std.
The illustrations for this book were rendered digitally.
Manufactured in the United States of America | 0818 FFG
First Simon & Schuster Books for Young Readers hardcover edition September 2018
2 4 6 8 10 9 7 5 3 1
Library of Congress Cataloging-in-Publication Data
Names: Calandrelli, Emily, author. | Weston, Tamson, author. | Illustrator. Kurilla, Renée,
Title: Ada Lace and the impossible mission / Emily Calandrelli with Tamson
Weston ; illustrated by Renée Kurilla.
Description: First Simon & Schuster Books for Young Readers paperback edition. |
New York : Simon & Schuster Books for Young Readers, 2018. |
Series: An Ada Lace adventure ; [4] | Summary: Eight-year-old Ada uses
new skills she learned from Milton to see if he sabotaged the social
studies project Nina and the two of them worked on together.
Identifiers: LCCN 2017043006| ISBN 9781534416857 (hardcover) |
ISBN 9781534416840 (pbk.) | ISBN 9781534416864 (eBook)
Subjects: | CYAC: Mystery and detective stories. | Schools—Fiction. | Behavior—Fiction.
Classification: LCC PZ7.1.C28 Aci 2018 | DDC [Fic]—dc23
LC record available at https://lccn.loc.gov/2017043006

Ada Lace

and the
Impossible Mission

Chapter One

Out of the Clink

Ada Lace. It concerns me to see you in detention," said Ms. Lily. "I know you love science, and your curiosity is admirable. But it has its limits. You can't just help yourself to school equipment after hours. Am I making myself clear?"

"Yes, Ms. Lily," said Ada.

"The rules are for everyone to follow. You don't get special treatment because your dad's a teacher here."

"I know, Ms. Lily. I didn't mean . . ." Ms. Lily held up her hand, and Ada closed her mouth. She'd always gotten along well with her principal. It didn't feel good to be in trouble with her.

"I know you know. But it doesn't hurt for you

to hear it from me. Now, let's make sure we don't meet like this again, okay?"

"Okay, Ms. Lily."

• • •

Milton was waiting outside. They had been on opposite sides of the room in the same detention.

"How come you didn't have to talk to her?" Ada asked.

"Aw, they're used to seeing me here. Stick with me, kid. They'll get used to you, too."

"No, thanks," said Ada. Ada and Milton hadn't been doing anything bad. Not really. They had just found a weird bug after school, and they used the science lab to dissect it. Ada had permission to be in the art room after school, with her dad, or outside, but all the other classrooms were off-limits.

"I never thought Ms. Azalea would turn us in. She's usually so nice!" said Ada.

"Yeah, but the risk is half the fun, right?" said Milton.

"Speak for yourself," said Ada. They got to the west entrance, near Mr. Lace's room. Milton was supposed to meet his mom outside.

"Wanna hang out later?" Milton asked.

"Nah, I have homework," said Ada, "and I'm not allowed to hang out today anyway."

"Tomorrow?"

"If Nina can come too."

"I guess," said Milton. Ada kept hoping that Milton and Nina would start to like each other more. It hadn't happened yet.

The worst part about trying to hang out with Nina and Milton at the same time was that they could never agree on anything. But Ada was determined to make it work. Usually that meant waiting until Nina and Milton both got tired of arguing, and suggesting something that they could agree on. Unfortunately, neither of them was that excited about the compromise. Ada suggested a movie instead of a water balloon toss (Milton) or creating a Juniper Garden swap shop (Nina). They agreed, and Ada was relieved. Then she realized they also had to agree on which movie to go see.

"But you've seen that *Wizards of Weird* movie," said Milton.

"I know! But it's totally rewatchable," said Nina.

"How do you know?" said Ada.

"I've seen it twice!" said Nina.

"Okay. Why don't we start with stuff we haven't seen?" Ada suggested.

That left *Teeny Tiny Kitten Frenzy*, which was too cute even for Nina, and *Mission Probable*. Usually Ada didn't like heist movies, but she decided to give it a try. Ada's mom brought them to the theater, and while Ada, Nina, and Milton watched their movie, Ms. Lace, Elliott, and Jack went to see *Teeny Tiny Kittens*.

"You guys are making such a big mistake," said Elliott. "Do you know how many kittens there are???"

"Uh, a lot?" said Ada.

"Five hundred and twenty-three!!!" said Elliott.

"Well, give me your review afterward, Elliott. Maybe I'll see it next time."

Ada was surprised at how much she enjoyed *Mission Probable*. It was pretty easy to figure out what was going to happen next. In fact, Nina kept leaning over to whisper to Ada what was coming up. But there was tech-nology Ada hadn't ever seen in a movie before. It was all kind of rough and homemade looking, which made it seem like a lot of it could be created at home. And some of the ways the thieves navigated the security were different from what she had seen in other movies. For example, instead of slinking around the security laser beams like ninjas, they used mirrors to divert the security beams *around them*. Nothing looked like it was something from the future. Instead, all their tools looked like something Mr. Peebles might be able to put together. It totally captured Ada's imagination.

"That was so cool, wasn't it?" said Milton.

"A little on the predictable side, don'tcha think?" said Nina.

"Oh, like seeing *W of W* for a third time?" said Milton. Nina rolled her eyes.

"Well, I thought all the tools were cool," said Ada.

"Yes! Exactly!" said Milton. "It makes heists look fun."

"Too bad they're so illegal," said Nina.

"Yeah," said Ada. "It is kind of too bad."

They met Elliott, Jack, and Ms. Lace outside the bathrooms.

"How was it, Ell?" Ada asked.

"A little disappointing," said Elliott. Ada was surprised.

"Why?"

"Well, first of all, there were only four hundred and ninety cats. I'm pretty sure they used some of the cats over again," said Elliott.

"And they weren't nearly as fuzzy as I was expecting," said Jack.

"So, thumbs down?" said Nina.

"Just wait for it to stream," said Elliott.

Later that night in bed, as Ada drifted off to sleep, she imagined she was scaling an unbelievably tall building using gecko gloves. She got to the top floor and looked in the window to see Milton. He smiled and waved. Then he opened the window, which tilted outward, and Ada was sent plunging down to the street below. She woke with a gasp. The noise woke George, who instantly played a lullaby. Ada drifted off to sleep again.

The next day in class, the students were assigned a social studies project. They were studying industries in the Bay Area, and the teacher had them work in pairs.

Their usual teacher, Ms. Grunflecker, was out on family leave and had been replaced by a substitute, Mr. Parable. He was okay, but he tried way too hard. It was amusing the first day when Mr. Parable wore a tie shaped like a slice of pizza. And then maybe the second day when he wore a fish tie. Then, on the third day, he moved on to a baseball bat tie. And after that they just kept rotating: pizza slice, fish, bat, pizza slice, fish, bat—always in that order. It took all the whimsy out of it.

He also had a parrot named Ferris Bueller in the classroom. That was fun at first too, but it got annoying really quickly. Every time Mr.

Parable asked a question, the parrot would shout, "I know! I know!" And Mr. Parable would say, "Bueller," then the bird would say, "I don't know." It was clear that Mr. Parable and Bueller had only ever taught for a week at a time. They ran out of material by the second week.

Even worse, if you left your desk to sharpen your pencil, the bird would say, "Have a seat! Have a seat!" And Mr. Parable would always take the bird's side!

Nina was much more tolerant of the sub, but even she started to complain when Mr. Parable assigned partners and she got Milton.

"I was that guy's biggest champion," said Nina, "and he sticks me with Milton? Doesn't he know who his friends are?"

"Oh, come on! Milton's not so bad," said Ada.

"You're just saying that because you guys are buddies now."

"Yeah, but doesn't that count?"

"I guess. . . ."

At dinner Ada complained to her mom about the parrot.

"His name's Ferris Bueller?" said Ms. Lace, laughing.

"Yeah. Why is that funny?"

"Oh, it's just from this great movie from the . . ."

"The nineties?" said Ada. She was usually interested in her parents' lives before she was born, but she was sick of Bueller.

"From the eighties, actually, Ada," said Mr. Lace. "And it wasn't that great a movie."

"Oh, come on! It's a classic!" said Ms. Lace.

"*Citizen Kane* is a classic," said Mr. Lace.

"Well, the parrot is annoying," said Ada.

"I have to agree with you there," said Mr. Lace.

That night, just as Ada was falling asleep, Milton called her on the ham. Ada's parents had rules about this: no calls after 8:30 p.m. She tried to ignore him, but Milton was persistent.

KD8PKR. KD8PKR. This is KD86E. Over.

KD8PKR! Pssssstttt! Ada? It's Milton.

Milton. What do you want? I'm trying to . . .

I have some great ideas for a heist!

Okay, well, good luck to you. I'm not a thief, and I'm not supposed to be . . .

Of course, it was then that Mr. Lace came in.

"Ada? What did we say about the radio? Good night, Milton," he said into the mic and clicked it off.

"I was trying to tell him, but . . ."

"You shouldn't even have the radio on after bedtime," said Mr. Lace.

"I forgot! I'm sorry."

"Next time, you're going to lose it for a week."

"It wasn't my fault!"

"Good night, Adita." He gave her a kiss on the forehead. "You know, I'm glad that you and Milton are getting along better, but you may want to set some limits for him."

"Yeah, I know," said Ada. "I can already feel the trouble starting to rub off on me."

"Well, we can't have that," Mr. Lace said as he closed Ada's door.

The next day during social studies, Ada's partner was missing. Mr. Parable told Ada that Pixie had strep throat and might not be in for the rest of the week.

"How about you work with Milton and Tina?"

"Nina!" both Ada and Nina said at the same time.

Ada was more annoyed by this name confusion than Nina was. Probably because Nina was relieved not to be working alone with Milton. Ada was concerned though. If she was trying to spend less time with Milton, this was not going to help.

Chapter Two
And Into the Garden Shed

Milton! We're not putting dead canaries in the mine. It's gross," said Nina. "And mean!"

"They wouldn't have to be real, Nina. Sheesh!"

They had been working on the project at Ada's house for two hours already, and three arguments had broken out. First Ada had to convince Nina that fortune-telling couldn't be considered a real industry in San Francisco. Then Milton suggested something that Ada thought was probably illegal. Finally they agreed to build a silver mine like the one at the Comstock Lode. It was in Nevada, but it sparked the silver rush and was a big part of San Francisco's development. Ada thought that she would have finished more of the project if she had been working by herself.

"She has a point, Milton. And Mr. Parable is clearly a bird lover. It could backfire on us."

"I'm just trying to give our viewers a sense of authenticity!" said Milton.

Ada knew what that meant. "Well, the miners had to go to the bathroom. Let's just put in a latrine. Is that authentic enough for you?"

"Now you're talking, Lace! I like how you think. I do, I do, I do!"

"Why do you encourage him?" asked Nina.

"It's called compromise, Neens."

It frightened Ada a little that she seemed to now understand how Milton's mind worked. But her strategy paid off, because the work went smoothly after that. They had built a replica of one of the mills, and, using Popsicle sticks, they had even re-created some of the square timbering developed by mining engineer Philip Deidesheimer. Nina came up with the idea of adding glitter to the miners' picks and lanterns. Even Milton was forced to agree that it was a nice touch. Despite their slow start, the project was coming together. Then Nina had to go feed her new pet rat, Templeton. When she was gone, Milton asked Ada if she wanted to learn some new heist skills.

"I learned how to pick a lock with two bobby pins. It's so fun! I could teach you," said Milton.

"This is totally going to get me in trouble," said Ada.

"No, no, no, absolutely not. I know just where to practice it," said Milton.

A little later Ada found herself with Milton at the shed in Juniper Garden. She was still not convinced it was a good idea.

"I don't know, Milton. The garden shed? I don't think the neighbors will like it," said Ada.

"It's no problem! My dad's stuff is in there. He's on the garden committee. I even have the key with me, just in case. But, you know, that would kind of defeat the purpose."

"Yeah, I get it."

Milton showed Ada how to insert two picks into the lock. One would start to turn the lock while the other would press against the little pins that kept it from turning.

"You just push against the pins inside until you find the sticky ones—the ones that don't

want to move easily. Then you push those up until they click."

Ada crouched next to Milton as he worked. She heard a series of clicks as the lock released. He opened the door.

"Wow! Can I try now?"

Ada had to try a couple of times, with no luck. But by the third attempt, the lock released and she opened the door.

"Hahahaha! That's so cool! I feel like a master spy!" she said, jumping up and down.

"What are you kids doing?"

Ada turned to find Ms. Reed standing behind her.

"I think you had better come with me," she said.

Ada agreed to clean out the shed to make up for breaking into it. She knew better than to argue with Ms. Reed. But that night she made clear to her parents that she hadn't done anything wrong—not really.

"Milton has a key. We were just playing around," said Ada.

"It's not that we don't believe you, Ade," said Ms. Lace. "I'm sure you weren't going to steal anything. But you can't just go around picking locks. It looks suspicious, and, as you can see, it gets you in trouble."

"Ada's in trouble!" Elliott said excitedly. "Are you going to put her in the spanking machine?"

"It hasn't come to that yet, Ell," said Mr. Lace.

"Why don't we ever get to use the spanking machine??!"

"We can try it out on you, if you want," said Mr. Lace.

"Nooo!!" Elliott ran and hid. The spanking machine wasn't real, of course—just a playful threat Ada's father liked to use. But Elliott was both fascinated and terrified by it.

After dinner Ada went to her room to start a journal entry that was due in a few days, but she was too upset. She was beginning to wonder if a friendship with Milton was worth it. He wasn't usually *bad* bad, but it was often too close for comfort. Ada had already gotten in trouble twice from hanging out with him. Just as she was about to turn off her ham radio, Milton came on.

KD8PKR. KD8PKR. KD86E here.

Sorry, KD86E, I'm out.

Ada clicked off the radio. Mr. Lace came in.

"Why don't I just keep this in my office for you for now," said Mr. Lace. "You can use it when you want, and then it won't get you into trouble at bedtime."

"Okay, Pop." She was actually a little relieved.

Chapter Three

That Old Milton Touch

They had just about finished the project when Nina and Milton got into another fight. This time they were at Milton's house.

"Just one miner," said Milton. "It totally happened, Nina. It's history!"

"No. No dead things, Milton. It's bad juju!" said Nina.

"Ugh, not that hooey again," said Milton.

"You won't be saying that when we fail," said Nina.

Ada didn't want to agree with Milton out loud, but she totally agreed with Milton.

"Milton, if we're not going to get a better grade by including bodies, then we shouldn't do it," said Ada.

"Fine," said Milton.

By the time they'd finished arguing, Nina had to go home to feed her rat.

"We can get to school early tomorrow morning, and I can help you finish then," said Nina. "I'm going to be in trouble if I don't leave now though."

"Go ahead, Nina," said Ada. "I'll make sure Milton keeps dead things out of the mine. And there's not that much left to do anyway."

"Are you sure?" said Nina. She was already shouldering her backpack on.

After Nina left, Ada realized that she was late too. Since her detention, Ada's parents had stricter rules about when she had to be home.

"I can finish up," said Milton. Ada was a little concerned.

"You better not get me into any more

trouble—not even just with Nina. Don't hide a stink bomb in there or something."

"No. No. No. Ada, really. I feel bad that I got you into trouble. Let me finish up the project." He seemed sincere. "I have an idea for how to do the square timbers quickly."

"Okay, Milton," she said. But she was still wary.

"I promise, no funny stuff. I just want you to know that you can trust me," said Milton.

That seemed particularly suspicious, but Ada was too late to argue.

The next day Ada met Nina and Milton a few minutes early for social studies. Milton brought the model. All the square set timbering had been finished, just as Milton promised.

"It looks great!" said Ada.

"I know! Best work I've done, if I do say so myself. Yes, yes, yes." Milton rubbed his hands together, admiring the replica. "There's no chance anyone's got a better project than ours, Ada. Especially now that it has the old Milton magic. It was great before, but now it's really something special."

"Get over yourself, Milton," said Nina.

"Wait. That old Milton magic?" Ada asked.

Mr. Parable came in before Ada had a chance

to find out exactly what Milton meant.

"Have a seat! Have a seat!" Bueller squawked.

"You heard the bird, Ava," said Mr. Parable.

"It's Ada!" said Ada.

Ada couldn't stop thinking about "that old Milton magic" all day. What did it mean, exactly? It could just be Milton being pleased with himself, which she had certainly seen before. But the more she thought about all the things that had happened recently, the more she began to worry. Milton liked pranks. Sure, so far they had been fairly harmless, but what if Milton had done something to their model? What if he put some figurines in there doing inappropriate things? What if he lined it with firecrackers? What if it exploded or collapsed or released noxious gas? They could wind up with an F, or worse—suspended. Or expelled! On the way to meet her dad in the art room, Ada ran her thoughts past Nina.

"Normally, I'd agree with you," said Nina. "But it's Milton's grade too. Do you really think he'd sabotage himself just for a laugh?"

"Gosh, who knows, Nina? But I don't think we can take the chance, do you?"

"I guess not."

The girls stopped by Mr. Parable's room before lunch to see if they could get their project back, but Mr. Parable was in a meeting. When they tried again after their last class, Mr. Parable had gone home for the day. The supply closet where he kept the projects was locked, and they weren't supposed to go into it without permission anyway.

"Drat!" said Ada. "We'll have to get it back from him tomorrow. I hope it's not too late."

But the next day, Tuesday, Mr. Parable had some kind of training, so an aide filled in. They had a substitute for a substitute! At lunch Ada asked Ms. Stead, the aide, if they could get into the supply closet, but she didn't have the key.

Ada gave it one final shot on Wednesday morning.

"Everyone has turned their projects in. I'm sorry, but I can't give you special treatment."

"But, Mr. Parable . . . ," said Ada.

"Your project looks wonderful, Ava. I don't know what you're worried about."

"It's Ada," she said. "A-D-A. *Ada*."

"I wouldn't be rude if I were you, young lady. I still haven't decided on your grade."

"I'm sorry, Mr. Peridittle," said Ada.

"What was that?"

"I'm sorry, Mr. Parable."

The Share Fair was just two days away. All the parents would be there and even the principal! Mr. Parable would give out their grades at the end. Ada would have to figure something out—and fast.

Chapter Four

ADA ASSEMBLES A TEAM . . . OF TWO

Ada hadn't spoken to Milton on the ham radio since before they turned the project in. She'd decided to lie low after the garden shed incident. They even did their work in the shed separately. But she needed to know what was up with the project, so she got permission to use her father's home office for a few minutes to talk to Milton. She practiced being persuasive before she picked up the mic, but as soon as she heard Milton's voice, she was filled with anger and desperation.

KD86E, this is KD8PKR. Are you there? Over.

This is KD86E. Ada! Hey! So I learned a new heist skill. Wanna hear about it? Over.

I can't talk long, Milton. I'm going to cut to the chase. What did you do to our project? Over.

What do you mean? I just fixed it! Maybe made a few extra enhancements. Over.

What kind of enhancements? Explosions? Fart sounds? Over.

Ha ha ha! That would be funny! Over.

No, it wouldn't be, Milton! You've gotten me in trouble twice. Now fess up! What did you do? Over.

Ada! I never meant to get you into trouble. Over.

Yeah, but somehow you always do. Over.

Hey, kid. I like to keep the people guessing! Over.

Milton. I don't feel like guessing. So why don't you just tell me what you did so I'll know what to expect. Or I may have to resort to something drastic. Over.

There was a long pause.

All right, Lace. I might have filled you in, but I don't like your tone. No. Nope. No, sirree. I think I'll let you find out on Friday with everyone else. Over and out.

KD86E? Milton! Grrrrrrrr.

It was time for plan B.

Ada turned the last few days over in her mind every which way. She and Milton had gotten along pretty well for a while. It had been fun. But she had never gotten in so much trouble before. She wasn't a bad kid! She was curious about stuff, sure. But that saying about curiosity killing the cat was a bunch of hooey. Curiosity *fed* the cat. Curiosity made the cat smarter and more interesting. Curiosity advanced catkind!

So what if she wanted to know how to pick a lock? So what if she thought that it was cool to figure out how to get into buildings in sneaky ways? Was that so wrong? She never meant to cause anyone any harm or commit any crimes or even really break any rules! She just liked to solve puzzles. When she thought about the stuff that got her in trouble, it wasn't her curiosity that was the problem, it was Milton. She was surely not going to let him get her in trouble again—not without a fight. So she had a plan. And without Milton to interfere, she knew she could pull it off.

But she would need an accomplice.

• • •

"We have to do what now?" asked Nina.

"Break into Mr. Parable's closet. We're going to have to make sure that project is squeaky clean. No pranks, no stunts, no gags. Nina, if that thing explodes in front of a roomful of parents in the middle of a Friday Share Fair, it's our butts on the line."

"But couldn't we just ask Mr. Parable if we can fix it?"

"I tried that! He said it wouldn't be fair to the rest of the class."

"Did you tell him Milton sabotaged it?"

"No . . . No, not exactly. I don't even know for sure that he did anything. But, let's face it, he's not above it, and, like I said, I'm not taking any chances. Luckily, we have a contingency."

"A plan B?"

"Yes, a plan B. Here's what I've got so far."

Ada rolled out a large sheet of paper that looked like a blueprint.

"Whoa, is that a picture of the school? How'd you get that?"

Ada shrugged. "I just downloaded it from the city website."

"So, what are we going to do? Tunnel underneath? Climb through the ductwork? Oh! I know. We're going to drop through a hatch in the roof, right? Better break out the gecko gloves."

"Uh, I hate to disappoint you, Nina. We're just going to go through the door."

Chapter Five
PLAN B

A few times after school, just for fun, Ada and Nina had used Ada's field guide to keep track of the habits of the staff and the students. Now these notes would come in handy.

Most of the staff left by 4:30 p.m. Ada's dad usually left by then too, but this Thursday he was staying late to grade some student projects. That meant Ada and Nina could also stay. Ms. Lily was the one wild card. Ada had never seen her leave before anyone else. Luckily, she usually kept to her office at the far south side of the school.

Ada and Nina were supposed to stay in Mr. Lace's room, in the west hallway just outside his door, or just outside the school. They weren't allowed to wander the building. Timing was crucial.

Mr. Lace would leave by 5:30 p.m. Ada and Nina would have to leave with him. Still, they couldn't enter Mr. Parable's classroom too soon, because there might be more teachers and staff hanging around. Ada figured they should head to Mr. Parable's room at 5:05 p.m. The janitor would be cleaning until after they had to leave, but, luckily, Ada had documented Mr. Bezzle's routine in her journal.

The school was laid out like a cross. Mr. Bezzle started at the farthest end of the north hallway and worked his way south until he reached the center of the school. Then he moved through the rooms in the east and west corridors and finished with the south hallway. On Thursdays he buffed the floors too, which meant that Ada and Nina would have plenty of time to make their way to Mr. Parable's room in the southern end of the school before Mr. Bezzle got there.

There were two obstacles that the girls had to get past before they could leave the west corridor and head toward Mr. Parable's room. The first was a security camera that was at the corner of the west hallway facing the entrance and Mr. Lace's classroom. The second was Mr. Parable's parrot, Bueller.

"Don't be mean to the parrot," said Nina.

"Don't worry, Nina," Ada said. "Sheesh. What kind of beast do you think I am?"

"I don't know! Maybe Milton's rubbed off on you!"

Ada wasn't sure whether Ms. Lily would be monitoring the security feed that closely after school, but she didn't want to take any chances. She would need to sabotage those cameras.

At first she considered using a jacket or a hat to cover the lens, but she thought it might be too hard to get it off afterward. Then Ada figured out she could shine a laser beam into the camera, filling the camera with light and distorting its view. The only problem was, they would have to be precise and quick—no small feat with nervous, shaky hands. If they missed the lens by a millimeter, the camera would see them.

Before they even dealt with the camera though, they would have to make sure that Bueller was asleep. Ada had a parabolic microphone, but it could capture sound only in open air or through a window. It would not work through a wall. They would have to go outside and listen through the classroom window to confirm that Bueller was sleeping. If he was awake, he might squawk and give away their presence to the janitor, Ada's father, or whoever else might be hanging around.

"Well, what if he's not asleep?" asked Nina.

"That'll be tricky," said Ava.

"Maybe we can bribe him into staying quiet. I could bring some cucumber slices? Or mango?"

"It's worth a try."

If the parrot was asleep, they would quickly sneak past the camera. Before continuing south to Mr. Parable's room, they would have to check to see if anyone was in the hallway nearby. Ada had taped a mirror to a selfie stick, so that before they turned and headed down the south hallway, they could extend it around the corner and use the reflection to see if the coast was clear. Then they would make their way to the second classroom on the left.

George would stand guard outside the door while they were inside working. If a janitor—or anyone else—approached, George would be programmed to ping the tablet Ada had connected him to, so that she and Nina could hide or get out of there quick.

"Well, what happens if someone notices George?" asked Nina.

"Hmmm . . . yeah. I hadn't thought about that. Could we camouflage him?"

"Yeah. Yeah, I think I know just what to do," said Nina.

The classroom might be locked, and they knew the supply closet would definitely be locked. Luckily, Ada had learned how to pick a lock.

"Milton taught you how to pick a lock?" said Nina. Ada hadn't told Nina. She already felt bad enough about getting in trouble. "Do I even want to ask?"

"It's just for fun!" Ada said. "There are tutorials for it online. I'll send you one."

Once they were in the classroom, Ada would turn on the light to the supply closet. This would require some preparation, because there were three switches on the wall of the classroom, and they had to be sure which was the correct one. If they turned on the classroom lights by accident, they would risk giving themselves away. Ada figured out that if she switched two off during school the next day, she could find out which one was for the closet.

After picking the lock with a bobby pin, they'd be in! Then they just had to examine the project for signs of Milton's sabotage, fix it, and leave.

"Sounds like a piece of cake," said Nina.

"That's the spirit!"

"I was kidding."

Chapter Six
THE FINAL PHASE

The next day at breakfast, Ada came down with her backpack loaded with all the tools she would need for her after-school caper: George, a tablet computer, the parabolic microphone, a laser pointer, and a few other just-in-case items.

Mr. Lace eyed her stuffed backpack curiously. "That's a big load you're carrying, Adita."

"Yeah, after we finish working on our schoolwork, Nina and I are going to tinker with George a little," said Ada.

Mr. Lace seemed a little confused, but then Ms. Lace handed him his coffee, and he didn't ask any more questions.

• • •

At school Ada tried to find a moment to figure out the lights in Mr. Parable's room, but whenever she got close, Mr. Parable always seemed to be standing right in front of the switches.

She got up to throw away trash, and Mr. Parable got up to consult the calendar next to the closet. She asked to go to the bathroom, and he was hanging something on the wall. When she returned to class and made her way toward the switches, there was Mr. Parable, hanging out in front of the closet.

Nina brought George's camouflage to lunch to show Ada.

"I made it last night," said Nina. She pulled out what looked like a beehive. Ada recognized it as a copy of the beehive the second-grade teacher had outside her classroom, right next to Mr. Parable's room. On the top it read, WE

ARE BUSY BEES. Ms. Janopolis put pictures of the second graders on it to show what they were working on.

"That's great, Nina," said Ada. "But don't we need to put pictures on it?"

"Yeah. I borrowed a couple this morning. I'll stick them on before we put it on George."

After lunch, Nina took a shot at the lights. First, she just spent an extra long time tying her shoe.

"Have a seat! Have a seat!" said Bueller.

"Nina?" said Mr. Parable. He looked at her pointedly over his glasses.

Nina wandered slowly toward her desk. When Mr. Parable turned around to speak to Casey Nesmith, Nina wandered back toward the door. Just as she got to the light switch, Bueller spoke up again.

"Have a seat! Have a seat!"

Mr. Parable turned back toward her. "Nina. Didn't I tell you to have a seat?"

Well, no, technically, Ada thought, but she didn't say so.

"Sorry, Mr. Parable," said Nina.

Nina took her seat and shrugged at Ada.

Then Mr. Parable told them that they would be watching a movie on immigration in nineteenth century California. Five minutes into the movie, Nina made her way to the trash can, just a few feet away from the supply closet. On her way back to her desk, she made an awkward loop toward the light switches. Ada was concerned it looked suspicious, but Mr. Parable didn't seem to notice. Not even Bueller mentioned it.

Ada saw Nina casually brush against the two switches closest to the closet door, in an attempt to turn them on. She didn't quite manage it the first time, so she stepped back and brushed against the switches again. She had to lunge forward a little bit and hunch down to get her shoulder under the switch. This time she managed to catch one switch but not the other. There wouldn't be a chance to try again—not now at least. She had turned on a light in the middle of the movie, and no one was happy about it. Mr. Parable paused the film.

"Nina Scarborough!" said Mr. Parable. "Am I

going to have to send you to see Ms. Lily?"

"No, Mr. Parable!" said Nina. "I'm sorry. It was an accident. It won't happen again."

Ada was surprised that Mr. Parable had remembered not just one, but both of Nina's names. As he was distracted by making sure that Nina made it to her seat, he flicked not just

the switch Nina had turned on but the one next to it too. He didn't notice, because the one he hit turned on the light in the closet, which was closed. Nina turned to Ada and winked. Ada had never been able to wink. She tried and just ended up crinkling her nose. That made her sneeze for some reason. Nina looked confused.

Milton caught up with Ada and Nina as they were heading toward Mr. Lace's room after school.

"You're sure you'll remember which one?" Nina asked Ada.

"Which one what?" asked Milton.

"Never mind, Milton," said Nina.

"Aw, come on! I can keep a secret," said Milton.

"There are no secrets, Milton," said Ada.

"And even if there were, you would be the last person . . ."

"Aha!" said Milton. "So, there is a secret."

"No!" said Nina. "No, there's not! We just wouldn't . . ."

"Suit yourself!" called Milton, walking away. "I can be a powerful ally . . . or enemy!"

"Great," said Ada under her breath.

"You sure we're doing the right thing?" asked Nina.

"Absolutely!" said Ada. She tried to sound as confident as she could. "And anyway, it's too late to change the plan now."

They sat in Mr. Lace's room working together until about 5:00 p.m. Then Ada gave the nod to Nina.

"Pop, Nina and I are just about finished.

We're going to go outside and play with George for a while."

Ada's father turned around and looked at her directly. "No wandering down hallways. No going to the vending machine without my supervision. You can go just outside, but not beyond the school yard entrance. Do you understand?"

His sternness almost threw Ada. She gathered her wits, swallowed, and answered him, "Yes, Dad. I understand."

As they left the room, Nina looked questioningly at Ada. Ada gave her a firm nod, and they went outside.

Chapter Seven

SABOTAGE

Ada and Nina got to Mr. Parable's window at 5:04 p.m. After scoping things out to make sure no one was watching, they crouched inside a group of hedges beneath the window and extended the parabolic mic above them on a little boom. The bird was still chattering—singing, actually.

"That's not good," said Ada.

"Well, wait a minute, listen to what he's singing," said Nina.

"Rock-a-bye, Bueller, on the treetop. . . ."

"You think he's singing himself to sleep?" asked Ada.

"Well, what else is that song for?"

They sat and listened for a full ten minutes. Bueller gradually got quieter and quieter, until they could barely hear him. Ada thought the bird would never go to sleep, then finally he did.

"Okay, let's roll," said Ada.

Nina tucked and somersaulted out of the bushes.

"I didn't mean literally," said Ada.

Nina shrugged.

Through the hedge they scanned the school yard to make sure no one was watching, then made their way quickly to the west side entrance.

Before they entered, Ada pulled out her laser pointer and turned it on. Nina opened the door as Ada aimed the laser pointer toward the camera. Ada's hands were shaking. She held the pointer with two hands to keep it as steady as possible, but she still wasn't sure she had it right on target. The only thing to do was to move quickly. So they darted past Mr. Lace's room just to the corner of the hall.

Ada could hear the floor polisher humming down at the north end of the school, which meant the janitor was still there, but that he was making quick progress—quicker than they had anticipated. Ada checked her watch: 5:18 p.m. They would have to hurry up. The noise might wake up Bueller, and they didn't want to risk letting the janitor get too close. They needed to be back to the art room before the janitor reached the south hallway.

Nina was about to make her way around the corner when Ada held her back. She reached into her backpack, pulled out the selfie stick with the mirror attached, and handed it to Nina as she continued to shine the laser into the camera. Nina extended the mirror past the corner and used it to look down the hall to either side. To the left they could see the janitor making his way north with the polisher. He had headphones on to block the noise—another plus. The hallway running south was empty. They had a clear path. Nina nodded to Ada, and they made their way toward the social studies room.

Once they reached Mr. Parable's door, Ada pulled George out of the backpack. She put him inside Nina's beehive, and they swapped him out for Ms. Janopolis's hive. Down the hallway, the floor buffer continued to hum away. The door to the classroom was unlocked. They brought the real hive inside with them, pulled the door shut, and crawled through the dark classroom to the closet door. Ada flicked the switch closest to the closet door. She pulled out two bobby pins and pushed them into the lock. After shifting them around a bit, the lock gave way with a louder than expected CLICK.

"Have a seat . . ." Bueller sighed. Ada and Nina looked at each other. Did birds talk in their sleep? They waited a full minute. Bueller was silent. Ada pointed to Nina and then pointed to her eyes and then the birdcage hanging by the teacher's desk. Nina nodded. She would watch the bird while Ada checked out their project.

Ada pushed the closet door open. On the shelves were ten clay, cardboard, and construction paper dioramas, mostly of ports, shops, and hotels. There was just one complex scale model

of a Comstock Lode silver mine. As beautiful as it looked on the outside, Ada was convinced something sinister lay hidden inside, and now she was about to find out what it was.

Ada pulled out a little flashlight to examine the model more closely. She noticed a couple of wires running underneath the rail system they had built that showed how the excess rock was carried away. She followed the wires with the flashlight beam to see where they led. Just then Nina appeared beside her in the closet.

"What's that?" she whispered, and reached for a switch the wires ran to.

"No, don't!" said Ada. But she was too late. Nina flicked the switch. Ada braced herself, waiting for an explosion, a foul odor, a chorus of

kazoos, or some combination of these. Instead, three little carts moved down the track inside the mine. When they reached the bottom, they rolled back up to the top again.

"Awww...," whispered Nina. "That's so cool. Milton wasn't being mean after all."

"Look here," said Ada. Buried in the square timbering in the mine were three little tiny tissue paper canaries, feet up.

"Figures," said Nina.

Suddenly, the hum of the floor buffer ceased. The janitor started to whistle "Three Little Birds."

"Oh no," said Ada. George couldn't resist that song.

Sure enough, George joined in.

Chapter Eight
MISSION COMPLETED

George was still connected to Ada's tablet. He pinged it, but they could hear the janitor's footsteps already coming toward Mr. Parable's room.

"Well, it's been fun," whispered Nina. "Now the jig is up. Time to pay our dues." Nina made for the door, but Ada stopped her. She was not ready to give up on her plan. She checked her watch. It was 5:26 p.m. Her dad would come

looking for them soon. They didn't have much time, but they had a couple of minutes.

Ada accessed George's controls on the tablet and sent him to the bathroom farther down the hallway. Ada and Nina crept out of the closet, and Ada carefully closed and locked the door. They slinked past Bueller and made their way to the door of the classroom. Ada heard the footsteps go past the door to Mr. Parable's room.

The janitor paused. George's song grew a little louder. Then the janitor continued walking faster. Ada snuck the mirrored stick out the door. The janitor had gone into the bathroom that George was in.

Ada and Nina seized the moment. They slipped through the door and down to the west hallway. They stationed themselves outside the art room door. It was 5:29 p.m.

"What about George?" said Nina.

"Don't worry," said Ada. She pulled out the tablet. She could see from George's video feed that he was tucked behind a radiator on the far side of the bathroom. Mr. Bezzle hadn't found him yet. She typed in a command and the song stopped. After a minute the janitor walked out looking confused and rejoined his floor buffer. When he was safely down the hallway, Ada called George back. He rolled happily down the hall to Ada. Just as they removed his costume and put it away, Mr. Lace walked out of the door.

"Boy, you girls are stealthy. I didn't even hear

you come back in!" said Mr. Lace. "I think I heard George though."

"Yeah, George can't resist a good song!" said Nina. She laughed for way too long. Ada looked at her. She stopped.

"You're looking a little pale, Nina," said Mr. Lace. "You should get to bed early tonight. After all, tomorrow's the big day, right?"

"Big day?" Nina asked.

"The Share Fair, right?" said Mr. Lace.

"Yes!" said both Nina and Ada, just a little too eagerly.

Shortly before midnight, Ada woke in a cold sweat. She realized she'd forgotten to shine the laser into the security camera on the way back to the art room. If anyone were to look back at the recording, it would show Ada and Nina slinking past like thieves. All she could do now was hope that Ms. Lily didn't review the tape. She didn't fall asleep until almost five in the morning.

The Share Fair had gone well. Ada, Nina, and Milton's project wowed everyone. They would have gotten A+, but Mr. Parable felt bad about the canaries, so he gave them an A.

"Beautiful work, you guys!" said Ms. Lace. "I'll see you tonight, Ade. I'm so proud of you!" Ada was exhausted and full of guilt.

And she felt really bad about Milton. He had done such great work, and she hadn't believed him. He was mischievous, but maybe not quite as bad as everyone thought.

"That fantastic little train almost makes me forgive you for the canaries, Milton," said Nina.

"Yeah, that was the idea," said Milton.

"So, you do have social skills," said Nina.

"Give him a break," said Ada. "Hasn't Milton been through enough?"

"Yeah!" said Milton. "Wait, what have I been through?"

"Oh, never mind," said Ada.

Nina whispered to Ada, "Ada, are you okay?"

"Yeah," said Ada. She wiped a bead of sweat off her forehead with the back of her hand.

"Okay, well, you better chill out a little or you're going to get us in trouble!"

Ada went through the rest of the day in a fog. What would happen if they found the footage from the hallway? If they found it three weeks from now, she would still probably be in trouble. Maybe even more trouble! To make matters worse, she heard Ms. Janapolis talking to Ms. Lily about how her hive was found in Mr. Parable's room. It was only a matter of time before Ada and Nina were caught. Would she ever be able to sleep again??

Finally, at 2:00 p.m., Ms. Lily called her to her office.

"Okay! Okay! I did it," Ada confessed.

"What? Did what?"

"I shined a laser into the security camera and snuck into the classroom! I just wanted to make sure Milton didn't ruin our project. And he didn't—he made it better. And now I just feel like a big jerk, and I'm sorry!"

"Oh, Nina," said Ms. Lily. "Well, I appreciate your honesty."

"So that's it?" asked Ada.

"Oh no. I'll be seeing you in detention again. For a week this time. But that wasn't why I called you down here."

"It wasn't?"

"No. I just wanted you to help with the kindergarten science fair."

Chapter Nine
Escape from the Gym

Ada was at the end of her week of detention. Nina got only two days, and she had already served it. It only seemed fair, since it was all Ada's idea and Ada's plan.

Milton met Ada outside of detention on the last day.

"I still can't believe you did a heist without me," said Milton.

"I did it *because* of you, Milton," said Ada. "And it turns out I was wrong—and bad at it. Why didn't you just tell me you put in that cool electric rail?"

"You were acting so nuts, I was kind of curious to see what you'd do," said Milton.

"Milton!" said Ada.

"I'm sorry!" said Milton. "I didn't think you'd take it so far. It's impressive! Anyway, I know you're in trouble now, but other than that, was it cool?"

"Oh, Milton. I'm a total amateur. So many mistakes were made!"

"Well, maybe you just need some practice," said Milton.

"I don't think so. I'm through getting in trouble," said Ada. "If there were someplace I had total permission to break in, complete a mission, and escape, I would do it. But that doesn't seem likely."

"Oh, Ada," said Milton. "I think you're onto something."

The next month Milton, Ada, and Nina, with Mr. Peebles's help, created a game idea called

Heist Room for the auditorium of the school. Heist teams were composed of no more than six participants and no fewer than three. Each team paid an entrance fee and could choose five tools to complete their mission. The proceeds would help purchase new microscopes for the school.

Inside the gym was a temporary mini building that Mr. Peebles, Mr. Bezzle, and a few other parent volunteers built. The teams were given a mission to break into the room, which was composed of smaller chambers, find the appropriate documents, and leave within fifteen minutes. The team with the fastest time won gift certificates to Moonberry frozen yogurt. Milton, Ada, and Nina had helped out a little with the planning, but they made sure that they didn't see any of the locks or interior chambers, so that they could participate.

Nina opted out of being Ada and Milton's third team member.

"I think I'll work with someone else for a change," she said.

Instead, Nina joined Elliott and his friend Jack.

"Wow," said Ada. "That's so nice of you!"

Then Milton said what Ada was thinking, "Too bad you're not going to win!"

"We'll see, Edison, we'll see," said Nina.

Ada and Milton let Mr. Lace be their third member.

Mr. Lace was the timekeeper, since Ada and Milton had more experience with locks. They got into the building fairly easily, but were surprised by how complicated it was to enter some of the chambers inside. In fact, as they cleared each chamber, there were progressively more locks to crack on the next one.

SiGN UP

Some of them were opened by solving a puzzle or solving a riddle, and the final chamber had a security system. Still, they were making good

time, and as the most experienced team they were confident of victory.

It was a big surprise to complete the mission and find Nina, Elliott, and Jack waiting for them.

"What took you guys so long?" said Nina.

"Yeah! How come you were such slowpokes??" said Elliott.

"Do they have ice cream at the yogurt place?" asked Jack.

"But . . . how . . . ?" asked Milton.

"Well . . . Huh . . . I guess Nina has some tricks up her sleeve," said Ada.

"Yeah, those videos you sent me were really helpful," said Nina.

Ada couldn't help but be proud of Nina for showing her up. She was also relieved to discover that crime wasn't her calling.

Behind the Science

LASER SECURITY SYSTEMS

Many schools, businesses, and homes have security systems that use lasers. A basic system would have a laser on one wall beaming at a sensor on another wall. The alarm won't go off as long as the laser continues to hit the sensor on the opposite wall. But if someone walks into the room and disrupts the laser, then for a brief moment the laser won't hit the sensor and—you better get moving—the alarm's going off! Typically, the lasers used in these types of security systems can't be seen with the naked eye—that would make it pretty easy for burglars to get around them. Instead, they might use infrared lasers, which look invisible to you and me. In the movie that Ada saw, the actors used mirrors to bounce the laser beam around them so that it would still hit the sensor while they walked into the room. In reality, this would be pretty hard to pull off. But, hey, that's movie magic!

Canaries in a Mine

The inside of mines can be very dangerous. In the early days miners could die not only from a poorly made cave collapsing, but also from toxic gases found deep in the ground, or even from a lack of oxygen in the air down in the mine. The especially scary part was that the miners couldn't immediately tell that the air they were breathing was dangerous—it wouldn't smell or look weird, so they would just keep on working. Only if a few of the miners died would anyone realize that there was carbon monoxide in the air or that there wasn't enough oxygen. So as a safety measure, miners started bringing canaries with them down into the mine. Canaries are small, so they're easy to carry. They're also constantly inhaling, so if there was anything dangerous in the air, a canary would pass out pretty quickly. This would be a sign to the miners that they should evacuate immediately. Today, we have better technology to test the quality of air, so thankfully, canaries are no longer used. But for the miners in the early nineteen hundreds, when there were no other options, they were a lifesaver!

LOCKS

Locks are used in so many different places in our lives—on your house, your locker, in hotels, and maybe on your personal field guide—and they can be all different types! Locks can be completely mechanical (like a traditional lock that requires a physical key) or electrical (like how the iPhone uses a fingerprint to unlock the screen), or a combination of both. You often can't tell by the outside of a lock, but there's a lot of science and engineering inside of it. If you ever want to see how cool a lock really is, you should Google pictures of a "clear lock" so you can watch the mechanical "guts" inside of it rotate, translate, shift, and click! Learning how to pick a lock is a fun way to learn how a lock works, but you should do this only with your parent's permission!

PARABOLIC MICROPHONES

A parabolic microphone is shaped like a large bowl and can be used to hear something that's far away from you. For example, bird-watchers can use parabolic microphones to listen to songs from birds that are perched up to two hundred feet away in a tree. The way it works is by gathering and focusing into a microphone sound waves coming from a single direction. These types of microphones are also used in sports like football so that newscasters can show viewers what coaches and players are saying on the field. In Ada's case, they're also great for spying and eavesdropping on a certain classroom parrot!

SELFIE STICK MIRROR

One clever way Ada was able to see around corners in the school was by attaching a mirror to a selfie stick. This is something you can try out at home! The way it works is simple geometry. You want the image of whatever you're trying to see to hit the mirror and then bounce into your eyes. You can practice this yourself by moving around a handheld mirror and discovering which objects you can see and which objects you can't! In Ada's case she wanted the hallway's image to hit her mirror and bounce into her eyes. You can get even more creative by connecting multiple mirrors together in order to see over or around things, like fences or walls. Mirrors can be a great tool for getting creative with exploring . . . or spying!

ESCAPE ROOMS

Ada and her friends designed the game Heist Room. These types of games exist in the real world and are typically called escape rooms. Escape rooms are a fun activity to do with family and friends. I've done a handful of them with my friends, and we love them! They're challenging, and you have to work as a team in order to escape the room. Most escape rooms have a theme—for example, "Escape jail!" or "Escape the haunted mansion!" or "Escape from the gym!" In order to "win," your group has to use clues scattered throughout the room to solve different puzzles. Usually one puzzle will lead to another, and another, and another. For one escape room, our group had to solve three different puzzles in order to get three different numbers that could be used on a combination lock. Once we had all the numbers, we could open the lock and escape the room! I have a feeling Ada, Nina, and Milton will try to find (or create!) more escape rooms in the future, don't you?

ACKNOWLEDGMENTS

Every kid should live life with a healthy dose of curiosity.

I'm thankful to my parents, who created an environment where curiosity was welcomed and encouraged. You made it okay to explore unknown territory, simply because it seemed interesting. You were encouraging when I wanted to pursue a career that you knew nothing about. You were supportive when I wanted to travel overseas by myself and live abroad in a foreign country. You've stood behind me as I've gone on countless adventures chasing the question "Wonder what that would be like?" You believed in my ability to pursue my curiosity, and for that I am grateful.

To my husband, Tommy, who is always down for random, spontaneous adventures. Thank you for giving me the confidence to pursue such curiosities as "Wonder what it's like to create a children's book series?"

To Kyell Thomas and Jennifer Keene at Octagon, thank you for challenging and widening my own curiosity when it comes to my career. You've helped me dream bigger and bolder.

And as always, thank you to Tamson Weston for clearly articulating Ada's curiosity about the world around her, to Renée Kurilla for beautifully bringing Ada's curiosities to life, and to Liz Kossnar for publishing Ada's curiosity to the world.

Turn the page for a peek
at another Ada Lace adventure in
Ada Lace and the Suspicious Artist.

Okay. A tick to the right," said Nina.

"I moved it to the right before, and you said to move it back," said Ada.

"Okay! Sorry! Wait a minute. Now I don't know if that background looks good with these pieces. Maybe we should start over."

"Nina!"

Ada was helping Nina build an online portfolio. It was the best way to introduce her creative energy to the universe, Nina had said. They had been at it all day, and patience was wearing thin. Ada had some of the coding skills, and Nina had a vision in her mind's eye, but making those two things meet in the middle was harder than they thought. All the numbers, letters, tags, and brackets were starting to blur together. They had already spent an hour trying to add a feature that would allow art lovers to position an image of the piece they were thinking of buying within a picture of their space so they could see what it would look like in context. Ada had learned a few different coding languages from working on George, but Web design was a different ball game. She couldn't quite manage what Nina wanted. And since Ada couldn't perfect the art placement feature, Nina seemed unhappy with everything.

"I'm sorry," said Nina. "It's just that I want Nina Nina Land to look professional . . . impressive. I want Guy Miroir to know I'm for real."

That was the other problem. Ada was sick of this Miroir character. Her mom had been preparing for his show all week, and Ada had never seen her so stressed out. Between Ms. Lace and Nina, it seemed like Miroir was the only important person in the world. She looked forward to having her friend and her mom back.

"I'm not a professional," said Ada. "If I were, I would be charging you!"

In the middle of it all Elliott burst into Ada's room with socks on his hands and started rubbing the corner of her desk, her bookshelf, and the head of her bed.

"What are you doing, Elliott?" asked Ada.

"I'm helping clean!" said Elliott.

Mr. Lace popped his head in. "Elliott. You're supposed to be cleaning *your* room."

"Oh, I am," said Elliott. "I'm just making it fun!"

"It's not supposed to be fun. It's supposed to be done!" said Mr. Lace.

Elliott stomped out of Ada's room.

"I don't know how much more I can do," said Ada. "At least right now. This is beyond my skill level."

"Fine," said Nina. "I'm going to go home for a bit and see if I can come up with something a little simpler, I guess."

"You know, Mr. Peebles's nephew, Tycho, is here," said Mr. Lace. "Isn't he a really good Web programmer?"

"Yes, he is!" said Ada. "Thanks, Dad."

Ms. Lace was at the gallery late again, so it was just Ada, Elliott, and Mr. Lace for dinner. Elliott insisted on cooking. It was his latest kick. Ada did not have high hopes. If she and Nina hadn't spent so much time together already, she would have gone to Nina's for dinner.

The table was set as only Elliott could set it—with a dinosaur in front of each plate. Ada sat in her usual seat.

"No, ADA! That's not your spot!" said Elliott. He was wearing a big poufy chef's hat and a gray apron that reached his toes.

"What do you mean? This is always my spot," said Ada.

"No, you're the *Stegosaurus*, obviously. *Dad's* the *Brachiosaurus*."

That did make sense somehow.

"But Dad's seat is always at the end," said Ada.

"Did *you* make dinner?" Elliott asked.

Ada sat behind the Stegosaurus. Elliott retreated into the kitchen. He came back out grasping a saucepan in two oversized, dirty yellow oven mitts. Just as he was about to reach

Ada's seat, he tripped over one of the apron's ties and tossed franks and beans over the whole table. Ada escaped almost unscathed, but for a few beans on her sweater. It was the perfect ending to a perfect day.

"OH NO!" yelled Elliott. "My masterpiece!"

Mr. Lace poked his head in and sighed.

"Mom just texted that she was on her way home," he said. "I'll tell her to bring a pizza from Donello's."

"I'm sorry, Dad," said Elliott.

"We'll try breakfast this weekend, Ell. And maybe we'll get you a better fitting apron."

An hour later they were seated around the pizza. Ms. Lace looked frazzled.

"I'm so glad to be here with you guys," said Ms. Lace.

"Bad day?" asked Ada.

"Well, it was challenging. Guy Miroir . . . needs a lot of things. He didn't like any of the hotels in the city, so we had to put him up in Napa Valley. He's very . . . particular. You know how these artists can be."

"Tell me about it," said Ada, thinking of Nina.

Looking for another great book?
Find it
IN THE MIDDLE.

Fun, fantastic books for kids
in the in-be**TWEEN** age.

IntheMiddleBooks.com

 SIMON & SCHUSTER
Children's Publishing   /SimonKids    @SimonKids